ANTONIO TABUCCHI

The Flying Creatures
of Fra Angelico

Translated from the Italian by Tim Parks

archipelago books

First published as *I volatili del Beato Angelico* by Sellerio editore in 1987.

Archipelago Books
232 3rd Street #AIII
Brooklyn, NY 11215

www.archipelagobooks.org

Library of Congress Cataloging-in-Publication Data
Tabucchi, Antonio, 1943–2012.
[Volatili del Beato Angelico. English]
The flying creatures of Fra Angelico/by Antonio Tabucchi ;
translated from the Italian by Tim Parks.—1st Archipelago Books ed.
p. cm.
"First published I volatili del Beato Angelico by Sellerio editore in 1987"—T.p. verso.
ISBN 978-1-935744-56-6
1. Short stories, Italian—Translations into English. I. Parks, Tim. II. Title.
PQ4880.A24V6513 2013
853'.914—dc22   2012025598

Distributed by Consortium Book Sales and Distribution
www.cbsd.com

Cover art: Hieronymus Bosch, detail from *The Garden of Earthly Delights*

The publication of *The Flying Creatures of Fra Angelico* was made possible
with support from Lannan Foundation, the National Endowment for
the Arts, the New York State Council on the Arts, a state agency,
and the New York City Department of Cultural Affairs.

Contents

Note

Hypochondria, insomnia, restlessness and yearning are the lame muses of these brief pages. I would have liked to call them *Extravaganzas*, not so much for their style, as because many of them seem to wander about in a strange outside that has no inside, like drifting splinters, survivors of some whole that never was. Alien to any orbit, I have the impression they navigate in familiar spaces whose geometry nevertheless remains a mystery; let's say domestic thickets: the interstitial zones of our daily having-to-be, or bumps on the surface of existence.

Then some of these pages, as for example "The Archives of Macao" and "Past Composed: Three Letters," are eccentric even on their own terms, refugees from the idea that originated them. To the extent that they are fragments of novels and stories, they are no more than meagre conjectures, or spurious projections of desire. They have a larval nature: they present themselves like creatures under formalin, with the oversize eyes of organisms still in the foetal stage – questioning eyes. But questioning whom? What do they want? I don't know if they're really questioning anyone, nor if they want anything, but I feel it would be kinder to ask nothing of them, since I believe that asking questions is the prerogative of those beings Nature has not brought to completion: it is that which is clearly incomplete that has the right to ask questions. Still, I cannot deny that I love them, these sketchy compositions entrusted to a notebook which out of an unconscious sort of faithfulness I have carried around with me constantly these last few years. In them, in the form of quasi-stories, are the murmurings and mutterings that have accompanied and still accompany me: outbursts, moods, little ecstasies, real or presumed emotions, grudges and regrets.

So that rather than quasi-stories, perhaps I should

say that these pages are no more than background noise in written form. Had I been a little more ruthless with myself, I would have called the collection *Buridan's Ass*. What stopped me from doing that, apart from a residual pride, which is often no more than a sublimated form of baseness, was the idea that although choice and completeness are not granted to the slothful wrapped up in their background noises, one is nevertheless still left with the chance of a few meagre words: so one may as well say them. A kind of awareness, this, not to be confused with noble stoicism, and not with resignation either.

A.T.

Some of these pieces have already been published in Italian or foreign reviews, though it would be difficult for me to supply an exact bibliography. All the same I would like to mention the original publications of two pieces which are linked to friends. Of the letters that make up "Past Composed," published in *Il cavallo di Troia*, no. 4, 1983–84, the one from Dom Sebastião of Portugal to Francisco Goya was dedicated to José Sasportes, and I would like to renew that dedication. "Message from the Half Dark" appeared in the catalogue (published by the Comune di Reggio Emilia, 1986) for a show of paintings by Davide Benati entitled *Terre d'ombre*. The piece is inspired by his paintings.

The Flying Creatures
of Fra Angelico

The Flying Creatures of Fra Angelico

The first creature arrived on a Thursday towards the end of June, at vespers, when all the monks were in the chapel for service. Privately, Fra Giovanni of Fiesole still thought of himself as Guidolino, the name he had left behind in the world when he came to the cloister. He was in the vegetable garden gathering onions, which was his job, since in abandoning the world he hadn't wanted to abandon the vocation of his father, Pietro, who was a vegetable gardener, and in the garden at San Marco he grew tomatoes, courgettes and onions. The onions were the red kind, with big heads, very sweet after you'd soaked them for an hour, though they made you cry a fair bit when you handled them. He was putting them in his frock gathered to form an apron, when he heard a voice calling: Guidolino. He raised his eyes and saw the bird. He saw it through onion tears filling his eyes and so stood gazing at it for a few moments, for the shape was magnified and distorted by his tears as though through a bizarre lens; he blinked his eyes to dry the lashes, then looked again.

It was a pinkish creature, soft looking, with small yellowish arms like a plucked chicken's, bony, and two feet which again were very lean with bulbous joints and calloused toes, like a turkey's. The face was that of an aged baby, but smooth, with two big black eyes and a hoary down instead of hair; and he watched as its arms floundered wearily, as if unable to stop itself making this repetitive movement, miming a flight that was no longer possible. It had got caught up in the branches of the pear tree, which were spiky and warty and at this time of year laden with pears, so that at every one of the creature's movements, a few ripe pears would fall and land splat on the clods beneath. There it hung, in a very uncomfortable position, feet straddled over two branches which must be hurting its groin, torso sideways and neck twisted, since otherwise it would have been forced to look up in the air. From the creature's shoulder blades, like incredible triangular sails, rose two enormous wings which covered the entire foliage of the tree and which moved in the breeze together with the leaves. They were made of different coloured feathers, ochre, yellow, deep blue, and an emerald green the colour of a kingfisher, and every now and then they opened like a fan, almost touching the ground, then closed again, in a flash, disappearing behind each other.

Fra Giovanni dried his eyes with the back of his hand and said: "Was it you called me?"

The bird shook his head and, pointing a claw like an index finger towards him, wagged it.

"Me?" asked Fra Giovanni, amazed.

The bird nodded.

"It was me calling me?" repeated Fra Giovanni.

This time the creature closed his eyes and then opened them again, to indicate yes once again; or perhaps out of tiredness, it was hard to say: because he was tired, you could see it in his face, in the heavy dark hollows around his eyes, and Fra Giovanni noticed that his forehead was beaded with sweat, a lattice of droplets, though they weren't dripping down; they evaporated in the evening breeze and then formed again.

Fra Giovanni looked at him and felt sorry for him and muttered: "You're overtired." The creature looked back with his big moist eyes, then closed his eyelids and wriggled a few feathers in his wings: a yellow feather, a green one and two blue ones, the latter three times in rapid succession. Fra Giovanni understood and said, spelling it out as one learning a code: "You've made a trip, it was too long." And then he asked: "Why do I understand what you say?" The creature opened his arms as far as his position allowed, as if to say, I haven't the faintest idea. So that Fra Giovanni concluded: "Obviously I understand you because I understand you." Then he said: "Now I'll help you get down."

Standing against a cherry tree at the bottom of the garden was a ladder. Fra Giovanni went and picked it up, and, holding it horizontally on his shoulders with his head between two rungs, carried it over to the pear tree, where he leaned it in such a way that the top of the ladder was near the creature's feet. Before climbing up, he slipped off his frock because the skirts cramped his movements, and draped it over a sage bush near the well. As he climbed up the rungs he looked down at his legs, which were lean and white with hardly any hairs, and it occurred to him they looked like the bird creature's. And he smiled, since likenesses do make one smile. Then, as he climbed, he realised his private part had slipped out of the slit in his drawers and that the creature was staring at it with astonished eyes, shocked and frightened. Fra Giovanni did himself up, straightened his drawers and said: "I'm sorry, it's something we humans have"; and for a moment he thought of Nerina, of a farmhouse near Siena many years before, a blonde girl and a straw rick. Then he said: 'Sometimes we manage to forget it, but it takes a lot of effort and a sense of the clouds above, because the flesh is heavy and forever pulling us earthwards.'

He grabbed the bird creature by the feet, freed him from the spikes of the pear tree, made sure that the down on his head didn't catch on the twigs, closed his wings, and then with the creature holding on to his back, brought him down to the ground.

The creature was droll: he couldn't walk. When he touched the ground he tottered, then fell on one side, and there he stayed, flailing about with his feet in the air like a sick chicken. Then he leaned on one arm and straightened his wings, rustling and whirling them like windmill sails, probably in an attempt to get up again. He didn't succeed, so Fra Giovanni gripped him under the armpits and pulled him up, and while he was holding the creature those frenetic feathers brushed back and forth across his face tickling him. Holding him almost suspended under these things that weren't quite armpits, he got him to walk, the way one does with a baby; and while they were walking, the creature's feathers opened and closed in a code Fra Giovanni understood, and asked him: 'What's this?' And he answered: 'This is earth, this is *the* earth.' And then, walking along the path through the garden, he explained that the earth was made of earth, and clods of soil, and that plants grew in the soil, such as tomatoes, courgettes and onions, for example.

When they reached the arches of the cloister, the creature stopped. He dug in his heels, stiffened and said he wouldn't go any farther. Fra Giovanni put him down on the granite bench against the wall and told him to wait; and the creature stayed there, leaning up against the wall, staring dreamily at the sky.

'He doesn't want to be inside,' explained Fra Giovanni to the father superior, 'he's never been inside; he says he's afraid of being in an enclosed space, he can't conceive of space if it's not open, he doesn't know what geometry is.' And he explained that only he, Fra Giovanni, could see the creature, no one else. Well, because that's how it was. The father superior, though only because he was a friend of Fra Giovanni's, might be able to hear the rustling of his wings, if he paid attention. And he asked: 'Can you hear?' And then he added that the creature was lost, had arrived from another dimension, wandering about;

there'd been three of them and they'd got lost, a small band of creatures cast adrift, they had roamed aimlessly through skies, through secret dimensions, until this one had fallen into the pear tree. And he added that they would have to shelter him for the night under something that prevented him from floating up again, since when darkness came the creature suffered from the force of ascension, something he was subject to, and if there was nothing to hold him down he would float off to wander about in the ether again like a splinter cast adrift, and they couldn't allow that to happen, they must offer the creature hospitality in the monastery, because in his way this creature was a pilgrim.

The father superior agreed and they tried to think what would be the best sort of shelter: something that was, yes, out in the open, but that would prevent any forced ascension. And so they took the garden netting that protected the vegetables from hedgehogs and moles; a net of hemp strings woven by the basket-weavers of Fiesole, who were very clever with wicker and yarn. They stretched the net over four poles which they set up at the bottom of the vegetable garden against the perimeter wall, so as to form a sort of open shed; and on the clods of earth, which the bird creature found so strange, they placed a layer of dry straw, and laid the creature on top of it. After rearranging his little body a few times, he found the position he wanted on his side. He sank down with intense pleasure and, surrendering to the tiredness he must have dragged after him across the skies, immediately fell asleep. Upon which the monks likewise went to bed.

The other two creatures arrived the following morning at dawn while Fra Giovanni was going out to check the guest's chicken run and see if he had slept well. Against the pink glow of the dawning day he saw them approaching in a low, slanting flight, as if desperately trying, and failing, to maintain height, veering in fearful zigzags, so that at first he thought they were going to crash against the perimeter wall. But they cleared it by a hair's breadth and then, unexpectedly, regained height. One hovered in the air like a dragonfly, then landed with legs wide apart on the wall. He sat there a moment, astride the wall, as if undecided whether to fall down on this side or the other, until at last he crashed down headfirst into the rosemary bushes in the flower bed. The second creature meanwhile turned in two spiralling loops, an acrobat's pirouette almost, like a strange ball, because he was a rolypoly sort of being without a lower part to his body, just a chubby bust ending in a greenish brushlike tail with thick, abundant plumage that must serve both as driving force and rudder. And like a ball he came down amongst the rows of lettuce, bouncing two or three times, so that what with his shape and greenish colour you would have thought he was a head of lettuce a bit bigger than the others off larking about thanks to some trick of nature.

For a moment Fra Giovanni was undecided as to whom he should go and help first. Then he chose the big dragonfly, because he seemed more in need, miserably caught as he was head down in the rosemary bushes, one leg sticking out and flailing about as if calling for help. When he went to pull him out he really did look like a big dragonfly, or at least that was the impression he gave; or rather, a large cricket, yes, that's what he looked like, so long and thin, and all gangly, with frail slender limbs you were afraid to touch in case they broke, almost translucent, pale green, like stems of unripe corn. And his chest was like a grasshopper's too, a wedge-shaped chest, pointed, without a scrap of flesh, just skin and bones: though there was the plumage, so sheer it almost seemed fur; golden; and the long shining hairs that sprouted from his skull were golden too, almost like hair, but not quite, and given the position of his body, head down, they were hiding his face.

Fearfully, Fra Giovanni stretched out an arm and pushed back the hair from the creature's face: first he saw two big eyes, so pale they looked like water, gazing in amazement, then a thin, handsome face with white skin and red cheeks. A woman's face, because the features were feminine, albeit on a strange insectlike body. 'You look like Nerina,' Fra Giovanni said, 'a girl I once knew called Nerina.' And he began to free the creature from the rosemary needles, carefully, because he was afraid of breaking the thing; and because he was afraid he might snap her wings, which looked exactly like a dragonfly's, but large and streamlined, transparent, bluish pink and gold with a very fine latticing, like a sail. He took the creature in his arms. She was fairly light, no heavier than a bundle of straw, and walking across the garden Fra Giovanni repeated what he had said the day before to the other creature; that this was the earth and that the earth was made of earth and of clods of soil and that in the soil grew plants, such as tomatoes, courgettes and onions, for example.

He laid the bird creature in the cage next to the guest already there, and then hurried to fetch the other little creature, the rolypoly one that had wound up in the lettuces. Though it now turned out that he wasn't as rounded as he had seemed, his body having in the meantime as it were unrolled, to show that he had the shape of a loop, or of a figure eight, though cut in half, since he was really no more than a bust terminating in a beautiful tail, and no bigger than a baby. Fra Giovanni picked him up and, repeating his explanations about the earth and the clods, took him to the cage, and when the others saw him coming they began to wriggle with excitement; Fra Giovanni put the little ball on the straw and watched with amazement as the creatures exchanged affectionate looks, patted each other's feet and brushed each other's feathers, talking and even laughing with their wings at the joy of being reunited.

Meanwhile dawn had passed, it was daytime, the sun was already hot, and afraid that the heat might bother their strange skins, Fra Giovanni sheltered one side of the cage with twigs; then, after asking if they needed anything else and telling them if they did to please be sure to call him with their rustling noise, he went off to dig up the onions he needed to make the soup for lunch.

That night the dragonfly came to visit him. Fra Giovanni was asleep, he saw the creature sitting on the stool of his cell and had the impression of waking with a start, whereas in fact he was already awake. There was a full moon, and bright moonlight projected the square of the window onto the brick floor. Fra Giovanni caught an intense odour of basil, so strong it gave him a sort of heady feeling. He sat on his bed and said: 'Is it you that smells of basil?' The creature laid one of her incredibly long fingers on her mouth as if to silence him and then came to him and embraced him. At which Fra Giovanni, confused by the night, by the smell of basil and by that pale face with the long hair, said: 'Nerina, it's you, I'm dreaming.' The creature smiled, and before leaving said with a rustle of wings: 'Tomorrow you must paint us, that's why we came.'

Fra Giovanni woke at dawn, as he always did, and straight after first prayers went out to the cage where the bird creatures were and chose the first model. A few days before, assisted by some of his brother monks, he had painted, in the twenty-third cell in the monastery, the crucifixion of Christ. He had asked his helpers to paint the background *verdaccio*, a mixture of ochre, black and vermilion, since he wanted this to be the colour of Mary's desperation as she points, petrified, at her crucified son. But now that he had this little round creature here, tail elusive as a flame, he thought that to lighten the virgin's grief and have her understand how her son's suffering was God's will, he would paint some divine beings who, as instruments of the heavenly plan, consented to bang the nails into Christ's hands and feet. He thus took the creature into the cell, set him down on a stool, on his stomach so that he looked as though he were in flight, and painted him like that at the corners of the cross, placing a hammer in his right hand to drive in the nails: and the monks who had frescoed the cell with him looked on in astonishment as with incredible rapidity his brush conjured up this strange creature from the shadows of the crucifixion, and with one voice they said: 'Oh!'

So the week passed with Fra Giovanni painting so much he even forgot to eat. He added another figure to an already completed fresco, the one in cell thirty-four, where he had already painted Christ praying in the Garden. The painting looked finished, as if there were no more space to fill; but he found a little corner above the trees to the right and there he painted the dragonfly with Nerina's face and the translucent golden wings. And in her hand he placed a chalice, so that she could offer it to Christ.

Then, last of all, he painted the bird creature who

had arrived first. He chose the wall in the corridor on the first floor, because he wanted a wide wall that could be seen from a good distance. First he painted a portico, with Corinthian columns and capitals, and then a glimpse of garden ending in a palisade. Finally he arranged the creature in a genuflecting pose, leaning him against a bench to prevent him from falling over; he had him cross his hands on his breast in a gesture of reverence and said to him: 'I'll cover you with a pink tunic, because your body is too ugly. I'll draw the Virgin tomorrow. You hang on this afternoon and then you can all go. I'm doing an Annunciation.'

By evening he had finished. Night was falling and he felt a little tired, and melancholy too, that melancholy that comes when something is finished and there is nothing left to do and the moment has passed. He went to the cage and found it empty. Just four or five feathers had got caught in the net and were twitching in the fresh wind coming down from the Fiesole hills. Fra Giovanni thought he could smell an intense odour of basil, but there was no basil in the garden. There were the onions that had been waiting to be picked for a week now and perhaps were already going off, soon they wouldn't be good enough for making soup anymore. So he set to pick them before they went rotten.

Past Composed: Three Letters

I

Letter from Dom Sebastião de Avis,[*] *King of Portugal,*
to Francisco Goya, painter

In this shadow world I inhabit, where the future is already present, I have heard tell that your hands are unrivalled in the depiction of carnage and caprice. Your home is Aragon, a land dear to me for its solitude, for the geometry

---

[*] Dom Sebastião de Avis (1554–78) was the last Portuguese king of the house of Avis. He came to the throne while still a child, was raised in the atmosphere of mysticism, and came to believe he had been chosen by God to accomplish great deeds. Nursing his dream to subject all Barbary to his rule and extend his kingdom as far as the

of its roads, for the quiet green of its courtyards hidden behind bellied gratings.

There are dark chapels with sorrowful portraits, relics, braids of hair in glass cases, phials of real tears and real blood; and small arenas where lithe men stalk the captive beast with the agile steps of dancers. Your land embodies some quintessential virtue of our peninsula in its lines, its faith, its fury. From these I shall choose some images for the symbol which, as heraldic emblem of a unique nation, you shall inscribe in the borders of the painting I hereby commission from you.

So then: On the right you shall paint the Sacred Heart of Our Lord. It will be dripping and bound in thorns, as in

revered Palestine, he put together a huge army, made up mostly of adventurers and beggars, and set off on a crusade that was to spell disaster for Portugal. In August 1578, exhausted by the heat and a forced march across the desert, the Portuguese army was destroyed by the light cavalry of the Moors near Alcácer-Quibir. Sebastião had left no direct descendants; with his death, Portugal was subjected to foreign domination for the first and only time in history. Annexed to the crown of Spain by Philip II, it regained its independence in 1640 after a national rebellion.

the images sold by pedlars and blind men in the squares outside our churches. But it must faithfully reproduce man's real anatomy, since to suffer on the cross Our Lord became a man, and His heart burst like a human heart and was pierced like any muscle of flesh. You shall paint it like that, muscular, throbbing, swollen with blood and pain, showing the lacework of the veins, the severed arteries, and the intricate latticework of the surrounding membrane open like a curtain and folded back like the peel of a fruit. It would be well to thrust the spear that transfixed it into the heart, the blade being shaped like a hook so as to tear open the wound from which His blood pours freely down.

On the opposite side of the painting, halfway up, and therefore level with the horizon, you shall paint a small bull. Paint him lying on his haunches, his front legs stretched out before him, like a pet dog; and his horns must be diabolical and his countenance evil. In the physiognomy of this monster you shall demonstrate that flair for the fantastical wherein you excel. Thus a sneer shall twist the animal's muzzle, but the eyes must be innocent, almost childlike. The weather shall be misty; the hour, dusk. The merciful, soft shadow of evening will already be falling, veiling the scene. The ground will be littered with corpses, thousands of corpses, thick as flies. You shall depict them as only you know how, incongruous and innocent as the dead always are. And beside the corpses, and in their arms, you shall paint the viols and guitars they took with them to their deaths.

In the middle of the painting, high up, amidst clouds and sky, you shall paint a ship. Not a ship drawn from life, but something from a dream, an apparition, a chimera. For this must be all the ships that took my people across foreign seas to distant coasts or down to the bottomless depths of the ocean, and again all the dreams my people dreamt looking out from the cliffs where my country runs to meet the sea, the monsters they conjured up in their imaginations, and the fables, the fish, the dazzling birds, the mourning and the mirages. And at the same time it shall also be my own dreams, the dreams I inherited from ancestors and my own silent folly. The figurehead of this ship shall have a human form and you must paint its features so that they seem alive and distantly recall my own. A smile may hover over them, but it must be faint, or vaguely mysterious: the incurable, subtle nostalgia of one who knows that all is vanity and that the winds which swell the sails of dreams are nothing but air, air, air.

II

Letter from Mademoiselle Lenormand, [*] *fortune-teller, to Dolores Ibarruri, revolutionary*

My cards portray ladies in sumptuous brocades, coffers, castles, and graceful dancing skeletons, not at all macabre and well suited to predict triumph and death to delicate princes and hot-tempered emperors. I do not know why they are asking me to read the story of your life, which has not yet begun and which, given the many years that

[*] Mademoiselle Lenormand was Napoleon's fortune-teller and one of the most celebrated French clairvoyants of her time.

separate it from this present time, I discern only through broad, perhaps deceptive, rents in the veil. Perhaps it is because, despite your humble birth, something in your destiny does partake of the nature of monarchs and lords: that profound sadness, like a fatal disease, of those who have the power to decide the fate of others, to dispose of men and women and to move, albeit for a noble end, poor human lives across the chessboard of destiny.

You will be born in the heart of Spain, in a village whose name is unclear to me, veiled in black gritty dust. Your father will plunge into the dark every morning at dawn, reappearing in the dead of night, heavy with filth and fatigue, to sleep like a rock in a bed near your own. Encased in the shell of her black dress, your mother will be silent and pious, terrified of what the future may bring. They will call you Dolores, out of Christian reverence, not realising that it foreshadows the nature of your life.

Your childhood will be utterly empty, I can see that clearly. You will not even wish for a doll, since never having seen one you will be unable to imagine such a thing, but simply cherish a vague longing for some kind of human shape onto which to transfer your childhood terrors. Your mother, poor ignorant woman, doesn't know how to stitch together a doll, doesn't realise that children need games, only that what they most need is food.

You will grow up with the righteous anger of the poor when they refuse to become resigned. You will speak to those the powerful think of as dirt and you will teach them not to become like your mother. You will kindle hope in them, and they will follow you. For how could the poor live without hope?

You will suffer the threats of judges, the beatings of the police, the coarseness of prison guards, the contempt of servants. But you will be beautiful, impetuous, fearless, blazing with scorn. They will call you 'La Pasionaria,' because of the fire that burns in your heart.

Then I see war. You will organise your people: on your side you will have the lowly and those who believe that men can be redeemed, and that will be your banner. You will even fight ideals similar to your own, because you consider them less perfect. And meanwhile the real enemy will defeat you. You will experience flight, exile, one hiding place after another. You will live on silence and scraps of bread, and at sunset the long straight roads will point to the horizons of lands as alien to you as those you are fleeing. Haylofts and stables, ditches, unknown comrades, people's compassion – these will be your shelter.

You are dark-haired and dark-eyed, a woman of the South, accustomed to blond, sun-drenched landscapes dotted here and there with the white of Don Quixote's windmills. You will find refuge in the great plains of the East, where the deep winter cold cracks both earth and hearts. Your voice has a resonant Latin cadence with syllables ringing like the clapping of hands: you speak a language made for guitars, for festivals in orange groves, for challenges in the arena where brave, stupid men grapple with the beast. The tongue of the steppes will sound barbaric, but you will have to use it and forget your own. They will give you a medal; every year, in early May, you will sit on a platform beside taciturn men, likewise wearing medals, to watch soldiers in dress uniform file by below, while the wind spreads the red of the flags and the thundering notes of martial anthems played by machines. You will be a veteran with a flat – reward in bricks and mortar for your heroism.

War again. Some are destined to witness death and destruction: you are one of them. In a city that will come to be called Stalingrad, death will snatch away the son you bore, the one real solace of your existence. My God, how quickly the years fly by in my cards, in your regrets! Only yesterday he was a child, and now he's a soldier already, and dead. You will be the heroic mother of a hero; your breast will bear another medal. The war is over now. Moscow. I see stealthy footsteps crossing the snow; a pure white blanket tries in vain to blur my cards; I sense the funereal gloom that pervades the city. At the carriage stops everyone stares at the ground to avoid meeting their neighbours' eyes.

And you too will be cautious, coming home of an evening, for this is a time of suspicion. At night you will wake with a start, soaked in sweat, unsure even of your own loyalty, since the worst heresy is to believe oneself in possession of the truth, and pride has brought down many. You will search your conscience long and hard.

And where have your old comrades gone meanwhile?
Vanished, all of them. You will toss and turn in your bed,
the sheets will be thorns. Outside it is bitterly cold; how
can the pillow burn so fiercely?

'All traitors?'

'Every one.'

'Even Francisco who laughed like a child and sang
the *romancero*?'

'Even Francisco.'

'Even El Campesino who wept with you over your
dead?'

Yes, even El Campesino – he's cleaning Moscow's toi-
lets now. And your short sleep will already be over. You
are sitting on your bed, eyes fixed on the opposite wall,
staring into the shadows (you always leave a night-light
on – you can't bear the darkness). But what else can you
do? South America is too far away, and besides, they won't
let La Pasionaria leave the friendly confines of Russia.

So you decide you had better cling to your ideals, make
of them an even stronger faith, stronger and stronger and

stronger still. And then after all, time is passing. Slowly, very slowly, but all things do pass. Men pass away, and suffering, and disasters. You too will almost be ready to pass away, and that will be a source of subtle, secret comfort. The meagre bun of your hair will turn white with age and grief. Your face will be dry, ascetic, with two deep hollows. Then your king will die too. You will take your place beside the coffin in the middle of the square, you will stay there day and night, always wholly yourself, silent, inflexible, your eyes always open, while a huge crowd files mutely by the embalmed corpse. Priestly, statuesque, carved in flint – 'That is La Pasionaria,' people will think when they see you, and here and there a father will point you out to his son. While all the time, to stop yourself giving way to the panic and longing which have carved out tunnels in your soul, the hands in your lap will be twisting and twisting your handkerchief, until you tie it into a knot (how strange, why are you stroking that little round wad?). And in your mind you see a room that time has borne away, a bare iron bed and a tiny Dolores, frightened and sick, with feverish eyes, calling plaintively, '*Mamaita, el jugete. Mamaita, por favor, el jugete.*' And your mother gets up from her chair and makes you something like a doll, knotting together the corners of her brown handkerchief.

Many more years await you, but they will all be the same. Dolores Ibarruri, when you look in your mirror what you will see will be the image of La Pasionaria, it will never change.

Then one day, perhaps, you will read my letter. Or you won't read it, but this will not have the slightest importance, because you will be old, and everything will already have been. Because if life could go back and be different from what has been, it would annihilate time and the succession of cause and effect that is life itself, and that would be absurd. And my cards, Dolores, cannot change what, since it has to be, has already been.

III

Letter from Calypso, a nymph, to Odysseus, King of Ithaca

Purple and swollen like secret flesh are the petals of Ogygia's flowers; brief showers, soft and warm, feed the bright green of her woods; no winter troubles the waters of her streams.

Barely the blink of an eye has passed since your departure, which seems so remote to you, and your voice calling farewell to me from the sea still wounds my divine hearing in this insuperable now. Every day I watch the sun's chariot race across the sky and I follow its course towards your west; I look at my white, unchanging hands; I trace a mark in the sand with a twig, as if adding a number to some futile reckoning, and then I erase it. And I have traced and erased many thousands of marks: the gesture is the same, the sand is the same, I am the same. And everything else.

But you live in change. Your hands have become bony, with protruding knuckles; the firm blue veins that ran across them have come to resemble the knotty rigging of your ship, and if a child plays with them, the blue ropes slither away under the skin and the child laughs and measures the smallness of his own small hand against your palm. Then you lift him down from your knees and set him on the ground, because a memory of long ago has caught up with you and a shadow crosses your face. But he runs around you, shouting happily, and at once you pick him up again and sit him on the table in front of you. Something deep, something that can't be put into words takes place, and intuitively you grasp the substance of time in the transmission of the flesh.

But what is the substance of time, and how can it come into being, if everything is fixed, unchanging, one? At night I gaze at the spaces between the stars, I see the boundless void, and what overwhelms you humans and sweeps you away is only one fixed moment here, without beginning or end.

Oh, Odysseus, to be able to escape this eternal green! To be able to follow the leaves as they yellow and fall, to live the moment with them! To discover myself mortal!

I envy your old age and I long for it; that is the form my

love for you takes. And I dream of another Calypso, old and grey and feeble, and I dream of feeling my strength dwindling, of sensing every day that I am a little closer to the Great Circle where everything returns and revolves, of scattering the atoms that make up this woman's body I call Calypso. And yet here I remain, staring at the sea as it ebbs and flows, feeling no more than its reflection, suffering this weariness of being that devours me and will never be appeased – and the empty terror of eternity.

The Passion of Dom Pedro

A man, a woman, passion and unreasoned revenge are the characters of this story. The white pebbled banks of the River Mondego where it flows beneath Coimbra provide the setting. Time, which as a concept is essential to the tale, is of little importance in chronological terms: for the record, however, I will say that we are halfway through the fourteenth century.

The opening scenario smacks of the banal. Marriages of convenience dictated by diplomacy and the need to establish alliances were banal in those times. Likewise banal was the young prince Dom Pedro sitting in his palace awaiting the arrival of his betrothed, a noblewoman from nearby Spain. And in banal fashion, as custom and tradition would have it, the nuptial delegation arrived: the future bride, her guards, her maids of honour. I would even venture to say that it was banal that the young prince should fall in love with one of the maids in waiting, the tender Inês de Castro, who in the manner of the time contemporary chroniclers and poets described as being slender of neck and rosy of cheek. Banal because, if it was common for a monarch to marry not a woman but a reason of state, it was equally common for him to satisfy his desires as a man with a woman to whom he was attracted for motives other than those of political convenience.

But the young Dom Pedro was a stubborn and determined monogamist; that is the first element in our story which is not banal. Fired by an exclusive and indivisible love for the tender Inês, Dom Pedro infringed the subtle canons of concealment and the prudent heedings of diplomacy. The marriage had been imposed on him for strictly dynastic reasons, and from a strictly dynastic point of view he did abide by it: but having produced the heir his father wanted of him, he moved together with Inês into a castle on the Mondego, and without marrying made her his real spouse: which is the second element in our story which is not banal. At this point the cold violence of reason enters the scene in the shape of a pitiless executioner. The old king was a wise and prudent man and in loving his son loved not so much the son himself as the king his son would become. He gathered together his councillors of the realm and they suggested a remedy they felt would settle the problem once and for all: the elimination of this obstacle to the good of the state. While the prince was away, Dona Inês was put to death by the sword, as a chronicler tells us, in her house in Coimbra.

Years went by. The legitimate queen had died some time ago. Then one day the old father died too and Dom Pedro was king. Now his vendetta could begin. At first it was a cruel and foul vendetta, but one which nevertheless still partook of human logic. With prodigious patience and the meticulousness of a solicitor's clerk, he had his police trace all of his father's old councillors. Some, already old and retired, were living quiet lives away from the public eye; others were difficult to find: plausible fears had prompted them to leave Portugal and offer their services to other monarchs. Dom Pedro waited for them one by one in the courtyard of his palace. He was haunted by insomnia. Some nights he would get up and break the unbearable silence of his rooms by having the servants light all the torches and by calling the trumpeters and ordering them to play. The chronicler of the period who recorded these events is prodigal with his details: he describes the bare, austere courtyard, the echoing of horses' hooves on stone, the rattle of chains, the shouts of the guards announcing the capture of another wanted man. He describes too how Dom Pedro waited patiently, standing motionless at a window from which he could look down on the courtyard and the road whence his victims must come. He was a tall man, very thin, with an ascetic face and long pointed beard, like a physician or a priest, and he always wore the same cloak over the same jerkin. Our meticulous chronicler even gives us the words, or rather supplications, the prisoners addressed to their torturer, and to which he never replied: for the king would do nothing more than supply details of a technical nature indicating what he felt would be the most fitting way to put an end to a victim's life. Dom Pedro was not without reserves of irony: for a prisoner called Coelho, which in Portuguese means 'rabbit,' he chose death over a gridiron. But in every case, and sometimes while they were still alive, he would have the victim's chest ripped open and the heart removed and brought to him on a copper tray. He would take the still warm organ in his hands and toss it to a pack of greedy dogs waiting below on the terrace.

But his bloody vendetta, which horrified our good chronicler, did not prove an effective placebo for Dom Pedro. His resentment at having been crushed by events now irremediable was not to be satisfied by the cardiac muscle of a few courtiers: in the stony loneliness of his palace he meditated a more subtle revenge which concerned not the pragmatic or human planes, but that of time itself and of the concatenation of events which make up our lives – events which in this case were already past. He decided to retrieve the irretrievable.

It was a hot Coimbra summer, and lavender and broom

were flourishing along the pebbly banks of the river. The washerwomen beat their laundry in the lazy trickle that snaked between the stones; and they sang. Dom Pedro realised that everything – his subjects, that river, the flowers, the songs, his very being there as a king – would have been the same even if everything had been different and nothing had happened; and that the tremendous plausibility of existence, inexorable as reality always is, was more solid than his ferocity, could not be wiped out by any vendetta of his. What exactly did the king think as he looked out of his window across the white plains of Portugal? What kind of sorrow was it that haunted him? The nostalgia for what has been may be heart-rending; but nostalgia for what we would have liked to happen, for what might have been and never was, must be intolerable. Probably it was this nostalgia that was crushing Dom Pedro. Every night, in his incurable insomnia, he would look up at the stars: and perhaps it was the interstellar distances, those spaces immeasurable in terms of human time which gave him the idea. Perhaps that subtle irony which he nursed in his heart along with the nostalgia for what hadn't been also played its part. In any event he thought up a brilliant plan.

As we have seen, Dom Pedro was a man of few words and strong character: the following morning a terse notice announced a great feast for the people throughout the kingdom, the coronation of a queen and a solemn nuptial procession in the midst of an exultant crowd all the way from Coimbra to Alcobaça. Dona Inês was exhumed from her tomb. The chronicler does not tell us whether she was already a bare skeleton or in what state of decomposition otherwise. She was dressed in white, crowned and placed on an open royal coach to the right of the king. The couple were pulled by a pair of white horses with big coloured plumes. Silver harness bells on the horses' heads jingled brightly at every step. The crowd, as ordered, followed on either side of the nuptial procession, marrying the reverence of subjects with their repugnance. I am inclined to believe that Dom Pedro, careless of appearances, from which anyway he was protected by the powers of a considerable imagination, was convinced he was riding, not with the corpse of his old lover, but with the real Inês before her death. One could maintain that he was essentially mad, but that would be an evident simplification.

It is eighty kilometers from Coimbra to Alcobaça. Dom Pedro came back alone and incognito from his imaginary honeymoon. Awaiting Donna Inês in the abbey at Alcobaça was a stone tomb the king had had sculpted by a famous artist. Opposite Inês's sarcophagus, on the lid of which she was shown in all her youthful beauty, and arranged *pied à pied*, so that come the day of judgement their residents would find themselves face-to-face, was a similar sarcophagus bearing the image of the king.

Dom Pedro was to wait many years before taking his place in the tomb he had prepared for himself. He passed this time fulfilling his kingly duties: he minted gold and silver coins, brought peace to his kingdom, chose a woman to brighten up his rooms; he was an exemplary father, a discreet and courteous friend, a fair administrator of justice. He even experienced happiness and gave parties. But these would seem to be irrelevant details. In all likelihood those years had a different rhythm for him than the rhythm of other men. They were all the same, and perhaps passed in a flash, as if they had already been.

Message from the Shadows

In these latitudes night falls suddenly, hard upon a fleeting
dusk that lasts but an instant, then the dark. I must live
only in that brief space of time, the rest of the day I don't
exist. Or rather, I am here, but it's as if I weren't, because
I'm elsewhere, in every place on earth, on the waters, in
the wind that swells the sails of ships, in the travellers
who cross the plain, in the city squares with their mer-
chants and their voices and the anonymous flow of the
crowd. It's difficult to say what my shadow world is made
of and what it means. It's like a dream you know you
are dreaming, that's where its truth lies: in its being real
beyond the real. Its structure is that of the iris, or rather
of fleeting gradations, already gone while still there, like

time in our lives. I have been granted the chance to go back over it, that time no longer mine which once was ours; it runs swiftly inside my eyes; so fast that I make out places and landscapes where we lived together, moments we shared, even our conversations of long ago, do you remember? We would talk about parks in Madrid, about a fisherman's house where we would have liked to live, about windmills and the rocky cliffs falling sheer into the sea one winter night when we ate bread soup, and of the chapel with the fishermen's votive offerings: madonnas with the faces of local women and castaways like puppets who save themselves from the waves by holding on to a beam of sunlight pouring down from the heavens. But all this flickers by inside my eyes and although I can decipher it and do so with minute exactness, it's so fast in its inexorable passage that it becomes just a colour: the mauve of morning in the highlands, the saffron of the fields, the indigo of a September night with the moon hung on the tree in the clearing outside the old house, the strong smell of the earth and your left breast that I loved more than the right, and life was there, calmed and measured out by the cricket who lived nearby, and that was the best night of all nights, liquid as the pulp of an apricot.

In the time of this infinitesimal infinite, which is the space between my now and our then, I wave you good-bye and I whistle 'Yesterday' and *'Guaglione.'* I've laid my pullover on the seat next to mine, the way I used to when we went to the cinema and I waited for you to come back with the peanuts.

'The phrase that follows this is false:
the phrase that precedes this is true'

Madras, 12 January 1985

Dear Mr Tabucchi,

Three years have gone by since we met at the Theosophical Society in Madras. I will admit that the place
was hardly the most propitious in which to strike up an
acquaintance. We barely had time for a brief conversation, you told me you were looking for someone and
writing a little diary about India. You seemed to be very
curious about onomastics; I remember you liking my
name and asking my permission to use it, albeit disguised,
in the book you were writing. I suspect that what interested you was not so much myself as two other things:

my distant Portuguese origins and the fact that I knew the works of Fernando Pessoa. Perhaps our conversation was somewhat eccentric: in fact its departure point was two adverbs used frequently in the West (*practically* and *actually*), from which we attempted to arrive at the mental states which preside over such adverbs. All of which led us, with a certain logic, to talk about pragmatism and transcendence, shifting the conversation, perhaps inevitably, to the plane of our respective religious beliefs. I remember your professing yourself to be, it seemed to me with a little embarrassment, an agnostic, and when I asked you to imagine how you might one day be reincarnated, you answered that if ever this were to happen you would doubtless return as a lame chicken. At first I thought you were Irish, perhaps because the Irish, more than the English, have their own special way of approaching the question of religion. I must say in all honesty that you made me suspicious. Usually Europeans who come to India can be divided into two groups: those who believe they have discovered transcendence and those who profess the most radical secularism. My impression was that you were mocking both attitudes, and in the end I didn't like that. We parted with a certain coldness. When you left I was sure your book, if you ever wrote it, would be one of those intolerable Western accounts which mix up folklore and misery in an incomprehensible India.

I admit I was wrong. Reading your *Indian Nocturne* prompted a number of considerations which led me to write you this letter. First of all I would like to say that if the theosopher in Chapter Six is in part a portrayal of myself, then it is a clever and even amusing portrait, albeit characterised by a severity I don't believe I deserve, but which I find plausible in the way you see me. But these are not, of course, the considerations that prompted me to write to you. Instead I would like to begin with a Hindu phrase which translated into your language goes more or less like this: The man who thinks he knows his (or his own?) life, in fact knows his (or his own?) death.

I have no doubt that *Indian Nocturne* is about appearances, and hence about death. The whole book is about death, especially the parts where it talks about photography, about the image, about the impossibility of finding what has been lost: time, people, one's own image, history (as understood by Western culture at least since Hegel, one of the most doltish philosophers, I think, that your culture has produced). But these parts of the book are also an initiation, of which some chapters form secret and mysterious steps. Every initiation is mysterious, there's no need to invoke Hindu philosophy here because Western religions believe in this mystery too (the Gospel). Faith is mysterious and in its own way a form of initiation. But I'm sure the most aware of Western artists do sense this mystery as we do. And in this regard, permit me to quote a statement by the composer Emmanuel Nunes, whom I had occasion to hear recently in Europe: '*Sur cette route infinie, qui les unit, furent bâties deux cités: la Musique et la Poésie. La première est née, en partie, de cet élan voyageur qui attire le Son vers le Verbe, de ce désir vital de sortir de soi-même, de la fascination de l'Autre, de l'aventure qui consiste à vouloir prendre possession d'un sens qui n'est pas le sien. La seconde jaillit de cette montée ou descente du Verbe vers sa propre origine, de ce besoin non moins vital de revisiter le lieu d'effroi où l'on passe du non-être à l'être.'*

But I would like to turn to the end of your book, the last chapter. During my most recent trip to Europe, after buying your book, I looked up a few newspapers for the simple curiosity of seeing what the literary critics thought about the end. I could not, of course, be exhaustive, but the few reviews I was able to read confirmed what I thought. It was evident that Western criticism could not interpret your book in anything but a Western manner. And that means through the tradition of the 'double,' Otto Rank, Conrad's *The Secret Sharer*, psychoanalysis, the literary 'game' and other such cultural categories characteristic of the West. It could hardly be otherwise. But I suspect that you wanted to say something different; and I also suspect that that evening in Madras when you confessed to knowing nothing about Hindu philosophy, you were – why, I don't know – lying (telling lies). As it is, I think you are familiar with Oriental gnosticism and with those Western thinkers who have followed the path of gnosticism. You are familiar with the Mandala, I'm sure, and have simply transferred it into your culture. In India the preferred symbol of wholeness is usually the Mandala (from the Latin *mundus*, in Sanskrit 'globe,' or 'ring'), and then the zero sign, and the mirror. The zero, which the West discovered in the fourth century after Christ, served in India as a symbol of Brahma and of Nirvana, matrix of everything and of nothing, light and dark; it was also an equivalent of the 'as if' of duality as described in the Upanishads. But let us take what for Westerners is a more comprehensible symbol: the mirror. Let us pick up a mirror and look at it. It gives us an identical reflection of ourselves, but inverting left and right. What is on the right is transposed to the left and vice versa with the result that the person looking at us is ourselves, but not the same self that another sees. In giving us our image inverted on the back-front axis, the mirror produces an effect that may even conceal a sort of sorcery: it looks at us from outside, but it is as if it were prying inside us; the sight of ourselves does not leave us indifferent, it intrigues and disturbs us as that of no other: the Taoist philosophers call it *the gaze returned*.

Allow me a logical leap which you perhaps will understand. We are looking at the gnosis of the Upanishads and the dialogues between Misargatta Maharaj and his disciples. Knowing the Self means discovering in ourselves that which is already ours, and discovering furthermore that there is no real difference between being in me and the universal wholeness. Buddhist gnosis goes a step further, beyond return: it nullifies the Self as well. Behind the last mask, the Self turns out to be absent.

I am reaching the conclusion of what, I appreciate, is an overly long letter, and probably an impertinence that our relationship hardly justifies. You will forgive me a last intrusion into your privacy, justified in part by the confession you made me that evening in Madras vis-à-vis your likely reincarnation, a confession I haven't the audacity to consider a mere whim. Even Hindu thinking, despite believing that the way of Karma is already written, maintains the secret hope that harmony of thought and mind may open paths different from those already assigned. I sincerely wish you a different incarnation from the one you foresaw. At least I hope it may be so.

I am, believe me, your

XAVIER JANATA MONROY

Dear Mr Janata Monroy,

Your letter touched me deeply. It demands a reply, a reply I fear will be considerably inferior to the one your letter postulates. First of all, may I thank you for allowing me to use part of your name for a character in my book; and furthermore for not taking offence at the novelistic portrayal of the theosopher of Madras for which you provided the inspiration. Writers are not to be trusted even when claiming to practise the most rigorous realism: as far as I am concerned, therefore, you should treat me with the maximum distrust.

You confer on my little book, and hence on the vision of the world which emerges from it, a religious profundity and a philosophical complexity which unfortunately I do not believe I possess. But, as the poet we both know says, 'Everything is worth the trouble if the spirit be not mean.' So that even my little book is worth the trouble, not so much for itself, but for what a broad spirit may read into it.

Still, books, as you know, are almost always bigger than ourselves. To speak of the person who wrote that book, I am obliged, in spite of myself, to descend to the anecdotal (I wouldn't dare to say biographical), which in my case is banal and low caste. The evening we made each other's acquaintance in the Theosophical Society, I had just survived a curious adventure. Many things had happened to me in Madras: I had had the good fortune to meet a number of people and to meditate on various strange stories. But what happened to me had to do with me alone. Thanks to the complicity of a temple guard, I had managed to get inside the compound of the temple of Shiva the Destroyer, which, as you know, is strictly forbidden to non-Hindus, my precise intention being to photograph the altars. Since you appreciate the meaning I attribute to photography, you will realise that this amounted to a double sacrilege, perhaps even a challenge, since Shiva the Destroyer is indentified with Death and with Time, is the *Bhoirava*, the Terror, and manifests himself in sixty-four forms, which the temple of Madras illustrates and which I wanted to photograph for myself. It was two in the afternoon, when the temple shuts its gates for siesta, so that the place was entirely deserted with the exception of a few lepers who sleep there and who paid not the slightest attention. I know this will arouse a profound sense of disapproval on your part, but I do not want to lie. The heat was oppressive, the big monsoon had only just finished and the compound was full of stagnant puddles. Swarms of flies and insects wandered about in the air, and the stench of excrement from the cows was unbearable. Opposite the altars to Shiva the traitor, beyond the troughs for the ablutions, is a small wall for votive offerings. I climbed upon it and began to take my photos. At that moment a piece of the wall I was standing on, being old and sodden with rain, collapsed. Of course I am giving you a 'pragmatic' explanation of what happened, since considered from another point of view the affair could have another explanation. In any event, when the wall crumbled I fell, skinning my right leg. A few hours later, when I'd got back to my hotel, the scratches had developed into an incredible swelling. It was only the following morning, though, that I decided to go to the doctor, partly because I hadn't had myself vaccinated at all before coming to India and I was afraid I might have got infected by tetanus – certainly my leg showed every sign that that was what it was. To my considerable amazement, the doctor refused to give me an anti-tetanus shot. He said it was superfluous since, as he said, tetanus runs its course much faster in India than in Europe, and 'if it were tetanus you would already be dead.' It was just 'a simple infection,' he said, and all I needed was some streptomycin. He seemed quite surprised that I hadn't been infected by tetanus, but evidently, he concluded, one occasionally came across Europeans who had a natural resistance.

I'm sure you will find my story ridiculous, but it's the story I have to tell. As far as your gnostic interpretation of my *Nocturne*, or rather of its conclusion, is concerned, allow me to insist in all sincerity that I am not familiar with the Mandala and that my knowledge of Hindu philosophy is vague and very approximate, consisting as it does in the summary found in a tourist guide and in a pocket paperback I picked up at the airport called *L'Induisme* (part of the 'Que sais-je?' series). As regards the question of the mirror, I started doing some hurried research only after getting your letter. For help I went to the books of a serious scholar, Professor Grazia Machianò, and am finding it hard work to grasp the basics of a philosophy of which I am woefully ignorant.

Finally I must say my own feeling is that on the most immediate level my Nocturne reflects a spiritual state which is far less profound than you so generously suppose. Private problems, of which I will spare you the tedious details, and then of course the business of finding myself in a continent so remote from my own world, had provoked an extremely strong sense of alienation towards everything: so much so that I no longer knew why I was there, what the point of my journey was, what sense there was in what I was doing or in what I myself might be. It was out of this alienation, perhaps, that my book sprang. In short, a misunderstanding. Evidently misunderstandings suit me. In confirmation of which allow me to send you this most recent book of mine, published a few days ago. You know Italian very well and may wish to take a look at it.

I am, believe me, your

ANTONIO TABUCCHI

Madras, 13 June 1985

Dear Mr Tabucchi,

My thanks for your letter and gift. I have just finished *Little Misunderstandings of No Importance* and your other book of short stories, *Reverse Side*, which you were generous enough to enclose. You did well, since the two complement each other and this made reading them more pleasant.

I am perfectly well aware that my letter caused you some embarrassment, just as I am also aware that you,

for reasons of your own, wish to elude the gnostic inter-
pretations that I have of your books and which you, as I
said, deny. As I mentioned in my first letter, Europeans
visiting India can usually be divided into two categories:
those who believe they have discovered transcendence
and those who profess the most radical secularism. I fear
that despite your search for a third way, you do fall into
these categories.

Forgive me my insistence. Even the philosophical position (may I so define it?) which you call 'Misunderstanding' corresponds, albeit dressed up in Western culture
(the Baroque), to the ancient Hindu precept that the
misunderstanding (the error of life) is equivalent to an
initiatory journey around the illusion of the real, that is,
around human life on earth. Everything is identical, as we
say; and it seems to me that you affirm the same thing,
even if you do so from a position of scepticism (are you
by any chance considered a pessimist?). But I would like
to abandon my culture for a moment and draw on yours
instead. Perhaps you will remember Epimenides' para-

dox which goes more or less like this: 'The phrase that follows this is false: the phrase that precedes this is true.' As you will have noticed, the two halves of the saying are mirrors of each other. Dusting off this paradox, an American mathematician, Richard Hoffstadter, author of a paper on Gödel's theorem, has recently called into question the whole Aristotelian-Cartesian logical dichotomy on which your culture is based and according to which every statement must be either true or false. This statement in fact can be simultaneously both true and false; and this because it refers to itself in the negative: it is a snake biting its own tail, or, to quote Hoffstadter's definition, 'a strange loop.'

Life too is a strange loop. We are back to Hinduism again. Do you at least agree on this much, Mr Tabucchi?

I am, believe me, your

XAVIER JANATA MONROY

Dear Mr Janata Monroy,

As usual your letter has obliged me to make a rapid and I fear superficial attempt to assimilate some culture. I only managed to track down something about the American mathematician you mention in one Italian periodical, a column written from the USA by journalist Sandro Stille. The article was very interesting and I have promised myself to look into the matter more deeply. I do not, however, know much about mathematical logic, nor perhaps about any kind of logic; indeed I believe I am the most illogical person I know, and hence I don't imagine I will make much progress in studies of this variety. Perhaps, as you say, life really is 'a strange loop.' It seems fair that each of us should understand this expression in the cultural context that best suits him.

But allow me to give you a piece of advice. Don't believe too readily in what writers say: they lie (tell lies) almost all the time. A novelist who writes in Spanish and who perhaps you are familiar with, Mario Vargas Llosa, has said that writing a story is a performance not unlike a strip-tease. Just as the girl undresses under an immodest spotlight revealing her secret charms, so the writer lays bare his intimate life to the public through his stories. Of course there are differences. What the writer reveals are not, like the uninhibited girl, his secret charms, but rather the spectres that haunt him, the ugliest parts of himself: his regrets, his guilt and his resentments. Another difference is that while in her performance the girl starts off dressed and ends up naked, in the case of the story the trajectory is inverted: the writer starts off naked and ends up dressed. Perhaps we writers are simply *afraid*. By all means consider us cowards and leave us to our private guilt, our private ghosts. The rest is clouds.

Yours

ANTONIO TABUCCHI

The Battle of San Romano

I would have liked to talk to you about the sky over Castile. The blue and the swift billowing clouds driven by the upland wind, and the monastery of Santa Maria de Huerta, on the road to Madrid, where I arrived one late spring afternoon to find Orson Welles shooting *Falstaff*, and it seemed to me the most natural thing in the world to come across that big bearded man with a cigar in his mouth, wearing a waistcoat and sitting on a stool in the Cistercian cloister. To tell you: Look, that's what I was like then, all those years ago, I liked Spain, *Hills Like White Elephants*, it was like pushing aside the cork curtain of a small rather dirty tavern and walking straight into a book by Hemingway, that was the door to life, it smacked of literature, like a page from *The Sun Also Rises*. It was a feast day, a holiday, I wasn't the person I am now, I still had the innocent lightness of someone who is waiting for things to happen; I could still take risks, write those stories, like *Dinner with Federico*, describing the limbo of adolescence, lazy afternoons, cicadas: small beer then, but it would take some courage now.

I was listening to a poet reading his poetry; 'my Southern Cross, my Hesperus,' and he was full of tenderness for a woman made of poetry, who in the end was himself. I sensed that he really did love this woman, because he loved her in the most authentic way possible, he loved himself in her, that is the real secret and in its own way a form of innocence, and I said to myself: Too late.

Nice place, the hotel, with blackened mirrors and ornamental picture frames, neoclassical columns made of wood, a discreet carefully selected audience of the kind one finds late evenings in luxury hotels, and me there listening with my heart beating, full of remorse and shame.

Why did he have the courage when I didn't, I wondered. What is this quality? Poetry, unawareness, awareness, or what? And then I saw this patient vehicle which has been transporting us for thousands of years. In a tray of food on the sideboard was an orange, our teacher used to say to us: Look, children, this is the world, that's how it's made, like an orange. The image floated up suddenly from the well of memory, and I looked on the surface of that orange for the long roads of Castile, and for a small car driving fast, thinking it could get into life through the little cork curtain of a page of Hemingway, and instead all I saw was orange peel, it had disappeared entirely from the fruit's surface. The poet read his fine poem with a fine, polished voice, I was on the point of tears, but not because of what he was saying (or rather, only partly because of that); no, it was me, it was because I couldn't find the road of that afternoon on the orange, the afternoon I saw Orson Welles, the afternoon I would have liked to talk to you about. So then I went up to my room to look at the enlargements I'd brought with me from the dark room. I'd broken down the painting piece by piece, dividing it into a fine grid, and I'd photographed every little square of the grid; it will be a long, exacting job requiring patience, interminable evenings with lens and lamp. Blown up by the enlargement process the surface of the frame is an epidermis full of wrinkles and scars, it almost makes you feel sorry for it, you see it was once a living organism, and now here it is in front of me like a corpse and I anatomise it to give it a sense it has lost with the passage of time, and which perhaps is not the original sense, the same way I try to give meaning to that afternoon on the road to Madrid, and I know the sense I'm giving it is different, because it had its real sense only then, in that moment, when I didn't know what sense it had, and now when I give it a sense made up of youth, prints of Spain and novels of Hemingway, it's just the interpretation of the person I am now: after its fashion, a fake.

This story, whose first-person narrator must of course be taken to be a fictional character, owes much to the observations of two art historians apropos of two panels of Paolo Uccello's triptych, *The Battle of San Romano*, one of which is in the National Gallery, the other in the Louvre. Of the first, which shows Niccolò da Tolentino leading the Florentines, P. Francastel (*Peinture et société*, Lyon, 1951) notes, upon analysing the spatial perspective, that Paolo Uccello simultaneously uses different perspectives, amongst them one elusive perspective close up and one 'compartmentalised' perspective in the background. The panel in the Louvre, which shows the part played by Micheletto da Cotignola, attracted the attention of A. Parronchi (*Studi su la dolce prospettiva*, Milan, 1964), again in response to problems of perspective. Parronchi examines the pictorial use of the silver leaves of the breastplates, and concludes that it is these which give the impression of reflections and of a multiplication of images. Basically the panel in the Louvre would seem to offer a way of playing with perspective already posited in Vitelione's *Perspectiva*; a method by which 'it is possible to arrange the mirror in such a way that the viewer sees in the air, outside the mirror, the image of something that is not within his field of vision.' In this way Paolo

Uccello's panel would appear to offer a representation not of real beings, but of ghosts.

The only other thing I need to say is that the author of this letter is writing to a female character.

Story of a Non-Existent Story

I have a non-existent novel whose story I would like to tell. The novel was called *Letters to Captain Nemo*, a title later altered to *No One Behind the Door*. I wrote it in 1977, I think, in two weeks of rough seclusion and rapture in a little village near Siena. I'm not sure what inspired me: partly memories, which in my mind are almost always mixed up with fantasy and as a result not very reliable; partly the urgency of fiction itself, which always carries a certain weight; and partly loneliness, which is often the writer's company. Without thinking much about it, I turned the story into a novel (a long short story) and sent it to a publisher, who found it perhaps rather too allusive, and a little elusive, and then from the point of view of a publisher, not very accessible or decipherable. I think he was right. To be quite frank, I don't know what its value in literary terms may or may not have been. I left it to settle for a while in a drawer, since I feel that obscurity and forgetfulness improve a story. Maybe I really did forget it. I came across it again a few years later, and finding it made a strange impression on me. It rose quite suddenly from the darkness of a dresser, from beneath the stacks of paper, like a submarine rising from obscure depths. I saw an obvious metaphor in this, a message almost (the novel was partly about a submarine); and as though in justification, or expiation (it is strange how novels can bring on guilt complexes), I felt the need to add a concluding note, the only thing that now remains of the whole and which still bears the title: *Beyond the End*. This would have been the winter of 1979, I think. I made a few small changes to the novel, then entrusted it to a publisher of a variety I thought might be more suitable for a difficult book like this. My choice turned out to be right, agreement was quickly reached and I promised delivery for the following autumn. Except that during the summer holidays I took the typescript with me in my suitcase. It had been alone for a long time and I felt it needed company. I read it again towards the end of August. I was by the Atlantic in an old house inhabited by wind and ghosts. These were not my ghosts, but real ghosts: pitiful presences which it took only the smallest amount of sensitivity or receptiveness to become aware of. And then I was particularly sensitive at the time because I knew the history of the house well and likewise the people who had lived there: by one of life's inexplicable coincidences my own life and theirs had become mixed up together. Meanwhile September came around bringing those violent sea storms that usher in the equinox; sometimes the house would be blacked out, the trees in the big garden waved their restless branches, and all night long the corridors echoed with the groans of ageing woodwork. Occasionally friends would come to dinner, the headlamps of their cars carving white swathes in the darkness. In front of the house was a cliff with a fearful drop straight into the seething waves. I was alone, I knew that for certain, and in the loneliness of existence the restless presences of the ghosts tried to make contact. But real conversations are impossible, you have to make do with bizarre, untranslatable codes, stratagems invented *ad hoc*. I could think of nothing better than to rely on a flashing light. There was a lighthouse on the other side of the bay. It sent out two beams and had four different time gaps. Using combinations of these variables I invented a mental language that was very approximate but good enough for basic conversation. Some nights I would suffer from insomnia. The old house had a big terrace and I would spend the night talking to the lighthouse, using it, that is, to transmit my messages, or to receive messages, depending on the situation, the whole exchange being orchestrated by myself, of course. But some things are easier than one imagines; for example, all you have to do is think: Tonight I'm transmitting; or: Tonight I'm receiving. And you're set.

I received many stories during those nights. I confess to transmitting very little. Most of the time I spent listening. Those presences were eager to talk and I sat and listened to their stories, trying to decipher communications which were often subject to interference, obscure and full of gaps. They were unhappy stories for the most part, that much I sensed quite clearly. Thus, amidst those silent dialogues, the autumn equinox came round. That day the sea was whipped up into a storm. I heard it thundering away from dawn on. In the afternoon an enormous force convulsed its bowels. Come evening, thick clouds had descended on the horizon and communication with my ghosts was lost. I went to the cliffs around two in the morning, having waited for the beam of the lighthouse in vain. The ocean was howling quite unbearably, as if full of voices and laments. I took my novel with me and consigned it to the wind page by page. I don't know if it was a tribute, a homage, a sacrifice or a penance.

Years have gone by, and now that story surfaces again from the obscurity of other dressers, other depths. I see it in black and white, the way I see things in dreams usually. Or in faded, extremely tenuous colours; and with a light mist all around, a thin veil that blurs and softens the edges. The screen it is projected on is the night sky of an Atlantic coast in front of an old house called São José de Guia. To those old walls, which no longer exist as I knew them, and to everybody who knew the house before I did and lived there, I duly dedicate this non-existent novel.

The Translation

It's a splendid day, you can be sure of that, indeed I'd say it was a summer's day, you can't mistake summer, I'm telling you, and I'm an expert. You want to know how I knew? Oh, well, it's easy, really, how can I put it? All you have to do is look at that yellow. What do I mean by that? Okay, now listen carefully, you know what yellow is? Yes, yellow, and when I say yellow I really do mean yellow, not red or white, but real yellow, precisely, yellow. That yellow over there on the right, that star-shaped patch of yellow opening across the countryside as if it were a leaf, a glow, something like that, of grass dried out by the heat, am I making myself clear?

That house looks as if it's right on top of the yellow, as if it were held up by yellow. It's strange one can see only a bit of it, just a part, I'd like to know more, I wonder who lives there, maybe that woman crossing the little bridge. It would be interesting to know where she's going, maybe she's following the gig, or perhaps it's a barouche, you can see it there near the two poplars in the background, on the left-hand side. She could be a widow, she's wearing black. And then she has a black umbrella too. Though she's using that to keep off the sun, because as I said, it's summer, no doubt about it. But now I'd like to talk about that bridge – that delicate little bridge – it's so graceful, all made of bricks, the supports go as far as the middle of the canal. You know what I think? Its grace has to do with that clever contrivance of wood and ropes that covers it, like the scaffolding of a cantilever. It looks like a toy for an intelligent child, you know those children who look like little grown-ups and are always playing with Meccano and things like that, you used to see them in respectable families, maybe not so much now, but you've got the idea. But it's all an illusion, because the way I see it that graceful little bridge, apparently meant to open considerately to let the boats on the canal go through, is really a very nasty trap. The old woman doesn't know, poor thing, she's got no idea at all, but now she's going to take another step and it'll be a fatal one, believe me, she's sure to put her foot on the treacherous mechanism, there'll be a soundless click, the ropes will tighten, the beams suspended cantilever fashion will close like jaws and she'll be caught inside like a mouse – if things go well, that is, because in a worst-case scenario all the bars that connect the beams, those poles there, rather sinister if you think abut it, will snap together, one right against the other with not a millimetre between and, wham, she'll be crushed flat as a pancake. The man driving the gig doesn't even realise, maybe he's deaf into the bargain, and then the woman's nothing to him, believe me, he's got other things to think about, if he's a farmer he'll be thinking of his vineyards, farmers never think about anything but the soil, they're pretty self-centred, for them the world ends along with their patch of ground; or if he's a vet, because he could be a vet too, he'll be thinking about some sick cow on the farm which must be back there somewhere, even if you can't see it, cows are more important than people for vets, everybody has his work in this world, what do you expect, and the others had better look out for themselves.

I'm sorry you still haven't understood, but if you make an effort I'm sure you'll get there, you're a smart person and it doesn't take much to work it out, or rather, maybe it does take a bit, but I think I've given you details enough; I'll repeat, probably all you have to do is connect together the pieces I've given you, in any event, look, the museum is about to close, see the custodian making signs to us, I can't bear these custodians, they give themselves such airs, really, but if you want let's come back tomorrow, in the end you don't have that much to do either, do you? and then Impressionism is charming, ah these Impressionists, so full of light, of colour, you almost get a smell of lavender from their paintings, oh yes, Provence . . . I've always had a soft spot for these landscapes, don't forget your stick, otherwise you'll get run over by some car or other, you put it down there, to the right, a bit farther, to the right, you're nearly there, remember, three paces to our left there's a step.

Happy People

'I'm afraid we're going to get bad weather this evening,' said the girl, and she pointed to a curtain of clouds on the horizon. She was skinny and angular, her hands moving jerkily, and she had her hair done up in a little ponytail. The terrace of the small restaurant looked out over the sea. To the right, beyond the screen of jasmine which climbed up to form a pergola, you could glimpse a little courtyard full of bric-à-brac, cases of empty bottles, a few broken chairs. To the left was a small ironwork gate, beneath which gleamed the little stairway carved into the sheer rock face. The waiter arrived with a tray of steaming shellfish. He was a little man with slicked-back hair and a shy manner. He put the tray down on the table and made a slight bow. On his right arm he carried a dirty napkin.

'I like this country,' said the girl to the man sitting opposite. 'The people are simple and kind.'

The man didn't answer; he unfolded his napkin, tucking it into the collar of his shirt, but then registered the girl's disapproving look at once and rearranged it on his knees. 'I don't like it,' he said. 'I don't understand the language. And then it's too hot. And then I don't like southern countries.'

The man was sixtyish, with a square face and thick eyebrows. But his mouth was pink and moist, with something soft about it.

The girl shrugged her shoulders. She seemed visibly annoyed, as if his confession contrasted somehow with her own candour. 'You're not being fair,' she said. 'They've paid for everything, the trip, the hotel. They couldn't have treated you with more respect.'

He waved his hand in a gesture of indifference. 'I didn't come for their country, I came for the conference. They treat me with great respect and I show mine by being here, so we're quits.' He concentrated on cracking open his lobster, making it plain there was nothing else to say about the matter. A small gust of wind blew away the paper napkin covering the bread basket. The sea was getting choppy and was deep deep blue.

The girl seemed put out, but maybe it was just a show. When she finally spoke it was in a tone of faint resentment, but with a hint of reconciliation too. 'You didn't even tell me what you'll be talking about, it's as if you wanted to keep me in the dark about everything, which isn't fair, I don't think.'

He had finally managed to overcome the resistance of his lobster and was now dipping the meat in mayonnaise. His face brightened and in a single breath, like a schoolboy parroting a lesson, he said: 'Structures and Distortions in Middle Latin and Vulgar Texts of the Pays d'Oc.'

The girl gulped, as if her food had gone down the wrong way, and she began to laugh. She laughed uncontrollably, covering her mouth with her napkin. 'Oh dear,' she hiccuped. 'Oh dear!'

He started to laugh too, but stopped himself because

he wasn't sure whether it was best for him to join in her outburst of hilarity or not. 'Explain,' he asked, when she had calmed down.

'Nothing,' the girl said, between intermittent giggles. 'It just occurred to me that you're rather better suited to the vulgar than the Middle Latin, that's all.'

He shook his head in fake pity, but you could see deep down he was flattered. 'In any event we can begin the lesson now; so listen carefully.' He held up a thumb and said: 'Point number one: you have to study the minor authors, it's the minor authors will make your career, all the greats have already been studied.' He raised another finger. 'Point number two: make the bibliography as long as you possibly can, taking care to disagree with scholars who are dead.' He raised yet another finger. 'Point number three: no fanciful methodologies, I know they're in fashion now, but they'll sink without a trace, stay with the straightforward and traditional.' She was listening carefully, concentrating hard. Perhaps the sketch of a timid objection was forming on her face, because he felt the need to offer an example. 'Think of that French specialist who came to talk about Racine and all Phaedra's complexes,' he said. 'A normal person, would you say?'

'What? Phaedra?' asked the girl, as though thinking of something else.

'The French specialist,' he said patiently.

The girl didn't answer.

'Quite,' he said. 'These days critics are in the habit of unloading their own neuroses onto literary texts. I had the courage to say as much and you saw how outraged everybody was.' He opened the menu and set about a careful choice of dessert. 'Psychoanalysis was the invention of a madman,' he concluded. 'Everybody knows that, but you try saying it out loud.'

The girl looked absent-mindedly at the sea. She had a resigned expression and was almost pretty. 'So what next?' she asked, still speaking as though her mind were elsewhere.

'I'll tell you that later,' said the man. 'Right now I want to say something else. You know what's positive about us, our winning card? Do you? It's that we're normal people, that's what.' He finally settled on a dessert and waved to the waiter. 'And now I'll tell you what's next,' he went on. 'What's next is, you apply for the place right now.'

'But we'll have your philologist friend against us,' she objected.

'Oh, him!' exclaimed the man. 'He'll keep quiet, he will, or rather, he'll be on our side, you'll see.' He left a pause that was full of mystery.

'When he walks down the corridor with his pipe and hair blowing about, you'd think he was God and Father himself,' she said. 'He can't bear me, he doesn't even say hello.'

'He'll learn to say hello, sweetie.'

'I told you not to call me sweetie, it brings me out in a rash.'

'In any event he'll learn to say hello,' he interrupted. He smiled with a sly look and poured himself some wine. He was doing it on purpose to increase the mystery and wanted it to be obvious he was doing it on purpose. 'I know all sorts of little things about him,' he finally said, letting a glimmer of light into the darkness.

'Tell me about them.'

'Oh, little things,' he muttered with affected casualness, 'certain escapades, old friendships with people in this country when it was not exactly a paragon of democracy. If I was a novelist I could write a story about it.'

'Oh, come on,' she said, 'I don't believe it. He's always in the front row when it comes to petitions and meetings, he's left-wing.'

The man seemed to think over the adjective she'd used. 'Left-handed, rather,' he concluded.

The girl laughed, shaking her head, which made her ponytail bob from side to side. 'In any event, we'll need support from someone from another university,' she said. 'We can't keep everything in the family.'

'I've thought of that too.'

'You think of everything, do you?'

'In all modesty . . .'

'Who?'

'No names.'

He smiled affably, took the girl's hand and assumed a

paternal manner. 'Listen carefully, you have to analyse people's motives, and that's just what I do. Everybody runs a mile from him, have you ever asked yourself why?'

The girl shook her head and he made a vague, mysterious gesture. 'There must be a reason,' he said.

'I've got a reason of my own,' she said. 'I'm pregnant.'

'Don't be stupid,' said the man with a cutting smile.

'Don't be stupid yourself,' the girl answered sharply.

The man had frozen with a slice of pineapple just an inch from his mouth; his face betrayed the surprise of someone who has recognised the truth.

'Since when?'

'Two months.'

'Why wait till now to tell me?'

'Because I didn't feel like it before,' she said firmly. She made a broad gesture which included the sea, the sky and the waiter who was arriving with the coffee. 'If it's a girl I'm going to call her Felicity,' she said with conviction.

The man slipped the pineapple into his mouth and swallowed in haste. 'A bit too passé and sentimental for my taste.'

'Okay, so Allegra, Joy, Serena, Hope, Letitia, Hilary, as you will. I don't care what you say, I think names have an influence on a person's character. Hear yourself called Hilary all the time and you begin to feel a bit hilarious, you laugh. I want a cheerful child.'

The man didn't answer. He turned to the waiter hovering patiently at a distance and made as if to write on his hand. The waiter understood and went into the restaurant to prepare the bill. There was a curtain of metal beads over the door which tinkled every time someone went in. The girl stood up and took hold of the man's hand, pulling him up.

'Come on, come and look at the sea, don't play the crotchety old fogy, this is the best day of your life.'

The man got up a little unwillingly, letting himself be pulled. The girl put her arm round his waist, pushing him on. 'It's you who looks pregnant,' she said. 'About six months, if you ask me.' She let out a ringing laugh and hopped like a little bird. They leaned on the wooden parapet. There were some agave plants in the small unkept piece of ground in front of the terrace and lots of wild flowers. The man took a cigarette from his pocket and slipped it between his lips. 'Oh God,' she said, 'not that unbearable stink again, it'll be the first thing I'll cut out of our life.'

'You just try,' he said with a sly look.

She held him tight against her, stroking his cheek with her head. 'This restaurant is delightful.'

The man patted his stomach. His expression was one of satisfaction and self-assurance. 'You have to know how to take life,' he answered.

The Archives of Macao

'Listen, my good man, your father has cancer of the pharynx, I can't leave the conference to operate on him tomorrow, I've invited half of Italy, do you understand? And then, with what he's got, a week isn't going to make much difference.'

'Actually our doctor says the operation should be done immediately, because it's a type of cancer that spreads extremely quickly.'

'Oh really, immediately indeed? And what am I supposed to say to the people coming to the conference, that I have to operate tomorrow and the conference is being postponed? Listen, your father will do what everybody else does, wait until the conference is finished.'

'You listen to me, Professor Piragine, I don't give a damn about your conference, I want my father to be operated on immediately, and any others too, if they're urgent.'

'I have no intention of discussing the schedule of my operating theatre with you. This is the University of Pisa and I am not just a doctor, I have well-defined teaching duties as well. I'm not going to put up with you telling me what I have to do. I can't operate on your father until next week; if that's not good enough, have the patient discharged and find another hospital. It goes without saying that the responsibility will be yours. Goodbye.'

The voice of the hostess invited the passengers to buckle their safety belts and extinguish their cigarettes, the stopover would last about forty minutes for refuelling and cleaning. And as through the window one began to see the lights of Bombay and a little later the blue lights of the runway, just then – it must have been due to the slight bump as the plane touched down, sometimes these things do spark off associations of ideas – I found myself on your scooter. You were driving with your arms out wide, because in those days the scooters used to have wide handlebars, and I was watching your scarf blowing in the wind. The fringe was tickling me and I wanted to scratch my nose but I was afraid of falling. It was 1956, I'm sure of that, because you bought the scooter as a celebration the same day I turned thirteen. I tapped two fingers on your shoulder, to ask you to slow down, and you turned, smiling, and as you turned the scarf slipped from your neck, very slowly, as if every movement of objects in space had been put into slow motion, and I saw that beneath your scarf you had a horrible wound slicing across your throat from one side to the other, so wide and open I could see the muscle tissue, the blood vessels, the carotid artery, the pharynx, but you didn't know you had the wound and you smiled unaware, and in fact you didn't have it, it was me seeing it there, it's strange how one sometimes finds oneself superimposing one memory over another, that was what I was doing. I was remembering how you were in 1956 and then adding the last image you were to leave me, almost thirty years later.

I appreciate one shouldn't write to the dead, but you know perfectly well that sometimes writing to the dead is an excuse, it's an elementary Freudian truth, because it's the quickest way of writing to oneself, and so forgive me, I am writing to myself, even though perhaps I am writing to the memory of you I keep inside me, the mark you left inside me, and hence in a certain sense I really am writing to you – but no, perhaps this too is an excuse, the truth is I am writing to no one but myself: even my memory of you, that mark you left inside me, is exclusively my business, you are nowhere and in nothing, there's just me, sitting here in this jumbo heading for Hong Kong and imagining I'm riding on a scooter, I thought I was on a scooter, I knew perfectly well I was flying on a plane that was taking me to Hong Kong from where I'll then take a boat to Macao, except that I was riding on a scooter, it was my thirteenth birthday, you were driving with your scarf around your neck and I was going to Macao by scooter. And without turning round, the fringe of your scarf in the wind tickling me, you shouted: To Macao? What on earth are you going to Macao for? And I said:

I'm going to look for some documents in the archives there, there's a municipal archive, and then the archive of an old school too, I'm going to look for some papers, some letters maybe, I'm not sure, basically some manuscripts of a symbolist poet, a strange man who lived in Macao for thirty-five years, he was an opium addict, he died in 1926, a Portuguese, called Camilo Pessanha, the family was originally from Genoa, his ancestor, a certain Pezagno, was in the service of the Portuguese king in 1300. He was a poet, he wrote only one little book of poems, *Clepsydra*, listen to this line: 'The wild roses have bloomed by mistake.' And you asked me: 'You think that makes any sense?'

Last Invitation

For the solitary traveller, admittedly rare but perhaps not implausible, who cannot resign himself to the luke-warm, standardised forms of hospitalised death which the modern statae guarantees and who, what's more, is terrorised at the thought of the hurried and impersonal treatment to which his unique body will be subjected during the obsequies, Lisbon still offers an admirable range of options for a noble suicide, together with the most decorous, solemn, zealous, polite and above all cheap organisations for dealing with what a successful suicide inevitably leaves behind it: the corpse.

Choosing a place suitable for a voluntary exit, and deciding on the manner of that exit, has become an almost hopeless undertaking these days, so much so that even the most eager are resigning themselves to natural forms of death, aided perhaps by the idea, now widespread in people's consciousness, that the atomic destruction of the planet, the Total Suicide, is just a question of time, and hence what's the point of taking so much trouble? This last idea is very much open to question, and if nothing else misleading in its cunning syllogism: first because it creates a connivance with Death and hence a sort of resignation to the so-called 'Inevitable' (a feeling necessarily alien to the exquisitely private act of suicide which can in no way be subjected to collectivist notions without its very essence being perverted); and second, even in the event of the Great Explosion, why on earth should this be considered a suicide, rather than a homicide inspired by destructive impulses towards others and the self carried out on a large scale and similar to those which inspired the wretched Nazis? And coercive in nature too, and hence in contrast with the inalienable nature of the act of suicide, which consists, as we know, in freedom of choice.

Furthermore, it has to be said that while waiting for the Total Suicide, people are still dying, a fact I consider worthy of reflection. And dying not just in the traditional and ancient fashions, but also and to a great extent as a result of factors connected with those same diabolical traps which foreshadow the Total Suicide. Such little inventions, for the solemn reason, amongst many others, that the cathode tubes of our houses must be on and that we must thus supply them with energy, are daily distributing their doses of poison which, being indiscriminate, are, if we wish to cavil, democratic; in short, while insinuating the idea of the inevitable Total Suicide, these things are all the time carrying out a systematic, constant and, I would even say, progressive form of homicide. Thus the potential suicide who does not kill himself because he might just as well wait for the Total Suicide, does not reflect, poor sucker, that in the meantime he is absorbing radioactive strontium, cesium and other delights of that ilk, and that while postponing his departure he is quite possibly already nursing in liver, lungs or spleen, one of the innumerable forms of cancer that the above-mentioned elements so prodigally produce.

In indicating a place where one might still kill oneself with dignity, in complete liberty and in ways esteemed by our ancestors and now apparently lost, one does not pretend to offer a public service (though it could be that), but to promote reflection, from a purely theoretical point of view, on a liberty: a hypothetical initiative practised upon ourselves which might be carried out without sinking to the more disheartening and vulgar stratagems to which the would-be suicide inevitably seems to be constrained in those countries defined as industrially advanced. (Obviously I am not referring to countries where problems of political, mental or physical survival exist and where suicide presents itself as a form of desperation and thus outside the realm of the kind of suicide here discussed, which is based on freedom of choice.)

From this point of view Lisbon would seem to be a city of considerable resources.

The first confirmation comes upon consultation of the telephone directory, where the undertakers fill a good sixteen pages. Sixteen pages in the Yellow Pages are a lot, you will have to agree, especially if one considers that Lisbon is not an enormous city; it is a first and very telling indication of the number of companies operating in the area, the only problem being that one is spoilt for choice. A second consideration is that death, in Portugal, does not appear to belong, as it does in other countries, to that ambiguous area of reticence and 'shame.' There is nothing shameful about dying, and death is justly considered a necessary fact of life; hence the arrangements which have to do with death get the same attention as other useful services to the citizen, such as *Águas*, *Restaurantes*, *Transportes*, *Teatros* (I mention a few at random), all services of public utility which can be contacted by phone. In line with this reasoning, the undertakers of Lisbon do not shun advertising: and in the telephone directory they advertise most forthrightly, with show, with pomp, and undeniable charm. Sober or ornate, and using extremely pertinent slogans, they will often take out a whole page to illustrate their services.

Some of them appeal to tradition: *'Há mais de meio*

século serve meis Lisboa' (has served half of Lisbon for more than half a century), boasts the advertisement of an undertaker based in Avenida Almirante Reis, and while the adjective *meio* referred to time seems to offer a purely historical piece of information, the *meia Lisboa* suggests something less statistically quantifiable, something warmer and more familiar; 'half of Lisbon,' in this case, means a majority, almost all, with slight connotations of classlessness. The dead of every social class and level, the announcement implies, are looked after by this traditional and implacable undertaker. Other undertakers, on the contrary, stress efficiency and modernisation. *'Os únicos auto-fúnebres automáticos'* (the only automatic hearses) claims an agency which boasts four branches covering the whole city. Modernity and mechanisation are powerful attractions, but this advertisement is certainly playing on the customer's curiosity. What on earth might automisation mean when applied to hearses? Worth checking out.

Almost all the undertakers also stress their experience and serious professional approach. To get this over, their ads in the Yellow Pages are accompanied by the faces of the proprietors and their staff: the unambiguous faces of undertakers with years of honest and respectable work behind them. What matters here is reliability, competence and the division of labour. These people don't disguise the physiognomy of their profession; on the contrary, they display the stereotype with pride. They have sorrowful but shrewd faces, long sideburns and often dark beards, very carefully trimmed. Their shoulders slope a little, they have black jackets, black ties and quite frequently glasses with heavy plastic frames. They know how to manage the business of death, that much is clear, that's what they've always done and they're proud of it. You can feel safe with undertakers like this.

But the most interesting advert for the potential customer comes from a discreet undertaker which stresses its *Serviço Permanente* and offers this copy line: '*Nos momentos difíceis a opção certa*' (The right choice at a difficult moment). Farther down in the ad, after the reassuring guarantee that the company uses only *flores naturais*, we have another line: '*Faça do nosso serviço um bom serviço, preferindo-nos'* (make our service a good service by choosing us). To whom can these lines be directed if not to the interested party him- or herself? The preferred target of this thoughtful undertaker is without doubt the man about to die. It is to *him* that the company wishes to talk, come to an understanding, achieve complicity. There is something of the conjugal in these bare and at the same time anodyne lines: they seem the quintessence of a contract, or a commonplace, they would be entirely plausible in the mouth of Emma Bovary's husband, in the evening in front of the fire. Or again in the mouths of any of us when we sit down to eat our dinner and set up a relationship of reciprocal connivance with what we call living.

Places to die, means of dying – they are so many and so varied one would need to write a whole treatise to cover them. I would rather leave the question up to the user, if only so as not to deprive suicide of that flair and creativity it ought to have. However, one can hardly avoid mentioning the means which, given the city's structure and topography, would seem to be Lisbon's chosen vocation: the leap. I appreciate that the void has always been a major attraction for spirits on the run. Even when he knows that the ground awaits him below, the man who chooses the void implies his refusal of fullness; he is terrified of the material world and desires to go the way of the Eternal Void, by falling for a few seconds through the physical void. Then the leap is also akin to flight; it involves a sort of rebellion against the human condition as biped; it tends towards space, towards vast distances, towards the horizon. Well, then, when it comes to this noble form of suicide, Lisbon is certainly the location par excellence. Hilly, constantly changing, riddled with stairways, sudden terraces, holes, drops, spaces that open all at once before you, complete with historic places for Historic suicides (try the Aqueducto das Águas Livres, the Castle, the Tower of Belém), sophisticated places for Art Deco suicides (the Elevador de Santa Justa) and mechanical places for Constructivist suicides (the Ponte 25 de Abril), this beautiful city offers the eager candidate a range of jumps unrivalled by any other European city. But the spot which lends itself more than any other to the leap is without a doubt the Cristo Rei on the banks of the Tagus. Undeniably this Christ is an invitation writ in stone, a sculptor's hymn in praise of the leap, a suggestion, a symbol, perhaps an allegory. This Christ offers us the very image of the *plongeur*, his arms outspread on a springboard from which he is ready to hurl himself. He's not an impostor, he's a companion, and that brings a certain comfort. Beneath flows the Tagus. Slow, calm, powerful. Ready to welcome the body of the volunteer and carry him down to the Atlantic, thus rendering superfluous even the most solicitous attentions of Lisbon's undertakers.

For brevity's sake I shall say nothing of other forms of suicide. But before I sign off, one at least, out of a sense of some duty to a whole culture, I must mention. It is an unusual and subtle form, it takes training, constancy, determination. It is death by *Saudade*, originally a category of the spirit, but also an attitude that you can learn if you really want to. The Lisbon city council has always made public benches available in appointed sites in the city: the quays by the harbour, the belvederes, the gardens which look out over the sea. Lots of people sit on them.

They sit silently, looking into the distance. What are they doing? They are practising *Saudade*. Try imitating them. Of course it's a difficult road to take, the effects are not immediate, sometimes you may have to be willing to wait many years. But death, as we all know, is that too.